"Song for a Scratchy Voice

Oh, my five bro — thers

ev-ery one ca-n sing the sweet-est

tune, but I have got a -

scrat-chy voice I sing just to my co-on.

A SONG FOR GAR

by Jean Merrill

Illustrated by Ronni Solbert

Did you ever sing the folk song "Barbary Allen" or "Big Rock Candy Mountain"? Everyone in the Marvell family loved these mountain songs and all six boys could sing them beautifully except Absolom, the youngest. He made up songs, but sang them only to his pet coon, named Barbary Allen. There was much arguing among the brothers because the oldest, Gar, was entering the Song Swapping contest and the prize was one hundred dollars — a lot of money. Everyone in the family had a suggestion. One day when Absolom was singing his own song to his pet coon, Gar overheard him. How do you think the people on Sour Cherry Ridge reacted when Gar sang it? You can try it, too — the words and music are in the book.

Classification and Dewey Decimal: Fiction (Fic)

About the Author:

JEAN MERRILL spent her growing years on a farm near Lake Ontario where she attended a one-room country school. A Phi Beta Kappa graduate from Allegheny College, she went on to do graduate work at Wellesley College where she received a Fulbright Scholarship for a year's study at the University of Madras in India. She held editorial positions with *Scholastic Magazine* in New York City, where she now makes her home. More recently she has turned to free-lance writing, doing film reviews, articles, children's books and a prize-winning television drama. Jean Merrill has traveled extensively through Europe and the Far East.

About the Illustrator:

RONNI SOLBERT, in addition to being a successful illustrator of children's books, is a recognized graphic artist, sculptress and painter. Born in Washington, D.C., she graduated with honors from Vassar College. She was granted a Fulbright Scholarship for study in India. She has done translating and broadcasting for the International Red Cross in Stockholm. Miss Solbert has traveled extensively. She now lives in New York City.

A SONG FOR GAR

for Chris

This edition lithographed in U.S.A. by Wetzel Brothers, Inc., Milwaukee, Wisconsin

by Jean Merrill

drawings by Ronni Solbert

1968 FIRST CADMUS EDITION
BY
E. M. HALE AND COMPANY
EAU CLAIRE, WISCONSIN

A SONG FOR GAR

ABSALOM MARVELL lived on Sour Cherry Ridge with his Ma and Pa, his five big brothers, and his own pet coon, named Barbary Allen. Absalom's brother Gar had brought the coon home to Absalom.

Next to Pa and Ma and his five brothers, Absalom thought more highly of Barbary Allen than anyone else in the world. He took her every place he went.

One spring morning when the wild-cherry blossoms were just coming on, Absalom lay in the grass singing to his coon.

Barbary Allen, what'll we do?
My brother Gar is mighty blue—

Absalom's voice was scratchy, and the tune didn't always go true as he planned it. Absalom's family laughed at his singing. For his Ma and Pa and his five brothers—every one—had a true sweet voice. The Marvells were known for their fine singing voices. All except Absalom. So he sang only to his coon.

Barbary Allen didn't mind Absalom's scratchy voice. When Absalom sang, she sometimes answered with a chittering coon sound.

Most mornings Absalom sang to Barbary Allen something like this:

> I sing to my coon
> And she answers me
> With a dillom-derry-down;
> My coon, she makes
> A chittering sound
> Like a dillom-derry-down.

It wasn't a song, really. It was more a kind of trifling talk that passed the time.

But this morning Absalom had no time for trifling. And what he sang to his coon was in the way of a serious question.

> Barbary Allen, what'll we do?
> What'll we do about Gar?

Absalom was worried about his brother Gar.

Gar was the oldest of Absalom's five big brothers. The brothers stood in this order: Gar, the oldest; then Geordie, Gavin, Ash, and Crandall. Absalom was the youngest.

Gar was powerful built like Pa Marvell. No man in the county could heft an axe like Gar.

Geordie was curly-headed, and favored his Ma's folk.

Gavin was a wonder with the rifle. No boy thereabouts could aim a rifle as true as Gavin.

Ash—he felt a song in his very toes. Ash would rather dance to a fiddle than anything in the world.

Crandall was the fastest growing. He bust out his boots so often he generally went entirely barefoot.

Absalom had his own pet coon.

"Six finer boys I couldn't want," Pa Marvell said.

"It would be pleasing to have one girl child, though," Ma Marvell sometimes said.

"Never you worry," Pa Marvell always replied. "Our six boys—every one of them—will one day bring home a wife. Then we'll have six fine girls as well."

It was this very thing that was a worry to Absalom.
For it was high time for his brother Gar to bring home
a wife and build his own cabin on Sour Cherry Ridge.
Gar had in mind a girl. A red-headed girl lived down
by Blue Mole Gap. Name of Camden Pride.

"I want no other girl," Gar said. "Camden Pride's
the one."

And Geordie and Gavin and Ash and Crandall and
Ma and Pa agreed that Camden Pride was surely the
girl for Gar. Absalom favored Camden Pride too.
For Camden had been heard to say Barbary Allen
was the smartest coon she ever had known.

Trouble was, Gar hadn't the money to fit out a
cabin of his own. Money came hard on Sour Cherry
Ridge. And Gar had none. Thinking on Camden
Pride and how he hadn't the money, Gar was as blue
as a boy could be.

"Barbary Allen, what'll we do?" Absalom sang again. But Barbary Allen was no help.

"The thing to do," Absalom said, "is to think of a song for Gar to sing."

For on Saturday night, there was to be a Song Swapping on Unity Hill. The boy who sang the likeliest song was to win a hundred-dollar purse.

Gar had asked his Ma and Pa and his five brothers to tickle their brains for the likeliest song he might sing. Everyone was to tell his notion of the likeliest song this very night.

Absalom wanted to help Gar. But the only song he knew any words to at all was a song called "Barbary Allen," the same name as his coon. It was a song Ma Marvell used to sing him every night when he was less than three years old.

But "Barbary Allen" was a song known to every singer in the county. So it wasn't a song to make people sit up and take notice. The only other songs Absalom knew were the made-up ones he sang to his coon.

> Barbary Allen, tell me a tune—
> Tell me a tune for Gar.

But Barbary Allen only made a chittering sound, and Absalom could think of no song. Absalom went along home to dinner, singing:

> My five brothers,
> Every one,
> Can sing the sweetest tune;
> But I have got
> A scratchy voice;
> I sing just to my coon.

AFTER DINNER, Absalom watched Gar take down the dulcimer Grandaddy Marvell had fashioned of fine pear wood when Gar was no higher than an axe handle. As Gar tuned the strings just so, Absalom felt near as blue as Gar. In a minute, Gar would ask Pa and Ma and his five brothers to name a song—and Absalom had not thought of one.

"Well," Gar said. "What shall I be singing at the Song Swapping?"

Pa spoke up first. "I recollect a song, Gar—a fighting song." And Pa sang out in his big, rumbling voice:

> Oh, the Martins and the Coys,
> They were reckless mountain boys,
> And they took up family feudin' when they'd meet—

"No," Ma interrupted Pa. "There's folks as don't hold with that kind of raring scrapping song."

"It's a man's song," Pa said. "A fighting song."

"It surely is that, Pa," Absalom said.

"So it may be," said Ma. "But it's not the kind of song a lady warms to. The way I reckon, the likeliest song is a song that will please every person as comes to the Song Swapping—man, woman, or child."

Geordie spoke up then. "Listen here, Gar," he said. "Here's what I allow to be the prettiest song in the world."

Absalom listened carefully, for Geordie had a light, clear tenor voice that would charm a coon down out of a tree. Geordie sang:

> Black is the color of my true love's hair;
> Her lips, her eyes are wondrous fair—

"No!" Gar shouted. "I cannot sing of a black-haired girl."

Gavin and Ash and Crandall laughed, and even Absalom could see that the red-headed Camden Pride would not find Geordie's song pleasing.

"It's a pretty song anyway, Geordie," Absalom said. "It's close to the prettiest song I ever heard."

Ash began to sing next. Bright as a blackbird he sang, and tapped his heels in time to the tune:

> My true love is a sun-burnt daisy—
> Ho-dee-ing-dong-doodle-alla-day.

Absalom felt—as he always did when Ash sang— like getting up and dancing. And when Ash went on:

> She won't work and I'm too lazy—
> Ho-dee-ing-dong-doodle-alla-day,

Absalom couldn't help joining in on the *ho-dee-ing* part, till Ash broke out laughing to hear that scratchy voice next to his own sweet one.

"Well, Ash," Ma said, "I admit that a song like that puts folks in a happy, *ho-dee-ing* frame of mind—even if it is purely on the trifling side. Myself, I favor a song with a serious notion in it."

Absalom guessed what Ma would sing. Ma would sing a hymn. Sure enough, Ma sang out in her high, pure voice:

> Jerusalem, the golden,
> With milk and honey blest—

"No question that's a fine song, Ma," Gar said. "Seems to me, though, it's more of a Sunday song than a tune for a Song Swapping."

"I agree," Gavin said. "Folks come to a Song Swapping to have their fancy tickled. I favor a fanciful song."

Gavin sang in his husky, teasing voice:

On that Big Rock Candy Mountain
The cops have wooden legs;
The bulldogs all have rubber teeth,
And the hens lay soft-boiled eggs.

Absalom chuckled at Gavin's song, for it surely was a fanciful kind of song. But Crandall didn't care so much for it.

"Something more on a funny song," Crandall said, and Crandall sang:

Oh, I went up in a balloon so big
The people on earth, they looked like a pig—
Like mice—like a katydid—like flieses
And like fleasens.

Absalom had to laugh out loud at Crandall's song.

But Pa said, "Who ever heard of a *fleasen?* A fighting song—that's the likeliest."

"A love song," Geordie said.

"A church song," Ma said.

"A dance tune," Ash said.

"Something like 'Big Rock Candy Mountain,'" Gavin said.

"No," Crandall said. "A funny song."

Absalom liked every song his Pa and Ma and his big brothers suggested. But he could see that not one of the songs was likely to please everybody. For that reason he spoke up.

The Big Rock Candy Mountain. By Permission Robbins Music Corporation.

14

"There's that 'Barbary Allen' song, Gar," he said. It was the only thing he knew to suggest at all.

Pa Marvell laughed. "Somehow that song reminds me of a coon."

But Gar said kindly, "I never can remember the words to that tune."

"It goes like this," Absalom said.

> In Scarlet town, where I was born,
> There was a fair maid dwellin'
> Made every youth cry, "Well-a-day!"
> Her name was Barbary Allen.

When Absalom sang, his Pa and Ma and his five brothers could not help laughing. For, pretty as the tune might be, Absalom's scratchy voice did not make it seem a very likely song.

"I reckon that tune's just too scratchy for a Song Swapping." Gavin grinned.

Absalom hid his face between his knees. He should have known better than to sing out beside his sweet-voiced brothers.

"Never you mind, Absalom," Gar said. "Scratchy voice or not, 'Barbary Allen' is a fair enough tune. And if it wasn't a tune so well known to every man, woman, and child in this county, I'd think it a very likely song to sing."

Absalom wished he could think of some other tune. But he could not. He could see Gar looked bluer than before. For what good was a Song Swapping with a hundred-dollar purse if his own family could not agree on the likeliest song?

"Never you worry, Gar," Pa said. "We're every one of us going to keep studying on it."

And everyone did. Gar thought on it as he cut logs for the cabin he wished to build for Camden Pride. Geordie studied on it as he toted water for Ma Marvell. Gavin considered as he tracked rabbits in the woods. Ash and Crandall argued about it as they hoed all day in the bean patch. Pa and Ma Marvell thought about it; and even Absalom, who scarcely knew any songs at all, thought about nothing else.

Trouble was, everybody's idea of a pleasing song was different. Saturday came, and still nobody had thought of a song for Gar to sing.

SATURDAY MORNING Absalom took Barbary Allen and climbed to the top of Sour Cherry Ridge, where he could see near the whole valley—all the way across to Blue Mole Gap, where Camden Pride lived. Many a puzzle had Absalom worried out in this very place. But he had never thought harder on anything than he was thinking this Saturday morning.

As he thought, he sang to Barbary Allen in his scratchy voice:

> I asked my coon
> Could she tell me
> The likeliest kind of song
> As Gar could sing
> If he wished to bring
> A red-headed girl along.
>
> Coon, she says, a dillom-down,
> This coon named Barbary Allen.

Absalom was thinking so hard on a song for Gar that he never noticed Gar himself coming along up the ridge. When Gar heard Absalom singing to his coon, he stopped and listened.

Absalom sang:

> I told my coon
> If Gar had a purse
> Of shining silver money,
> He'd use it all
> To fix a house
> For his red-headed honey.

Gar smiled at Absalom's song, partly because Absalom's voice was so scratchy and the tune didn't come out true as he planned it. And partly because what Absalom sang was the very truth.

Absalom went on singing:

> I told my coon
> The cherry tree
> With blossom now is bowed;
> If Heaven looks
> One half as fair,
> The good Lord must be proud.

Absalom never saw his brother Gar scrunched down behind a laurel bush, and he went on making up a song for his coon.

> I told my coon
> Jerusalem's
> A land of milk and honey,
> But Gar rather live
> On Sour Cherry Ridge
> And drink milk with his honey.

Gar looked across the valley to Blue Mole Gap. For he couldn't help thinking of Camden Pride.

Absalom hummed to himself a bit.   Then he sang
again:

> I asked my coon
> What makes a boy
> Go rarin' round the town,
> And what makes a boy
> Want to yell and scrap
> And knock the other boys down.
>
> Coon, she says, a red-headed girl,
> A dillom-derry-down.

Gar smashed his fist on the ground.   A man surely
did feel like rarin' round when he couldn't bring home
the girl he'd a mind to.

Absalom's song ran on:

> "Oh, coon," I said,
> "I'm mighty glad
> To have a coon like you,
> For a coon won't tease
> A boy like a girl,
> Won't make a boy feel blue."

Gar chuckled to himself.

Absalom sang:

> "Oh, coon," I said,
> "If you marry me,
> We'll raise the cutest chaps—
> For it wouldn't s'prise me
> If our kids were born
> A-wearing coonskin caps!"

Gar like to bust out laughing when Absalom sang about the coonskin caps in that scratchy voice.   But he bit down hard on a laurel twig so Absalom wouldn't hear him.   And when Absalom gathered up Barbary Allen and started along down the ridge, Gar followed a careful piece behind, and Absalom never had a notion Gar was on the ridge at all.

"Cuss you, coon," Absalom said.   "Here I trifle away the whole morning singing to you, and I have not thought of a song for Gar."

IN THE EVENING, Pa and Ma and Absalom and his five brothers climbed into the spring wagon to drive to the Song Swapping.

"Well, Gar," Pa asked, "what song do you reckon to sing?"

"I truly don't know," said Gar.

"You sing 'Big Rock Candy Mountain,' boy," Gavin said. "That's a sure song."

"Sing a funny song, Gar," Crandall begged.

"I favor a love song," Geordie said. "Love songs are pleasing to young girls."

"Menfolk like a fighting song," Pa said.

Absalom, riding on the back of the wagon, didn't say anything. Gar, all scrubbed his smartest, looked worried.

"Never you worry, Gar," Ma said as they came to Unity Hill, where half the county was come to hear the Song Swapping. "You got the sweet Marvell voice, and anything you sing is bound to please some folks."

Gar went off then to sit with the other boys who'd come to try their luck for the hundred-dollar purse. Absalom went with his Pa and Ma and Geordie, Gavin, Ash, and Crandall to sit where they could hear.

Then the Song Swapping started. Many were the songs as were sung. There were love songs and fighting songs, dance songs and hymn tunes. Every kind of song you could think of.

The young girls smiled at the love songs, and the menfolk stomped for the fighting songs. Some folks nodded at the sad and serious songs. The gay fellows clapped for the dance songs, and the children laughed at the funny ones.

At last it was Gar's turn. He took his place and tuned his dulcimer just so.

"I hope he sings a dance tune," Ash whispered.

"I hope it's a love song," Geordie said.

"Sssh," Ma said. For Gar was commencing to sing.

First Gar sketched out the beginning of the tune on the dulcimer, and nobody could be sure whether it was going to be a gay song or a serious song. Then Gar smiled and began to sing.

Everybody listened, quiet as could be. For it was a song nobody had heard before. That is, nobody but Absalom. For Gar was singing, in his sweet, true Marvell voice:

> I asked my coon
> Could she tell me
> The likeliest kind of song
> As I could sing
> If I wished to bring
> A red-headed girl along.
>
> Coon, she says, a dillom-down,
> This coon named Barbary Allen.
>
> I told my coon
> If I had a purse
> Of shining silver money,
> I'd use it all
> To fix a house
> For my red-headed honey.
>
> Coon, she says, a dillom-down,
> This coon named Barbary Allen.

"It's a love song," Geordie whispered.

I ASKED MY COON

(All the words for Gar's song)

Tune: "Polly-Wolly-Doodle"

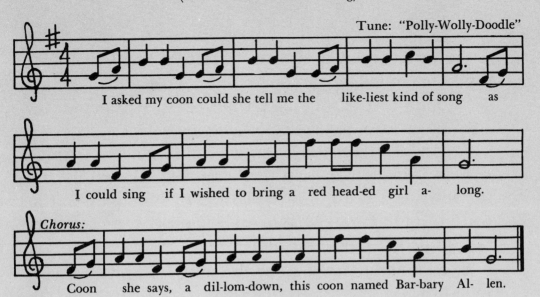

I asked my coon could she tell me the like-liest kind of song as

I could sing if I wished to bring a red head-ed girl a- long.

Chorus:

Coon she says, a dil-lom-down, this coon named Bar-bary Al- len.

2 I told my coon
If I had a purse
Of shining silver money,
I'd use it all
To fix a house
For my red-headed honey.

3 I told my coon
The cherry tree
With blossom now is bowed;
If Heaven looks
One half as fair,
The good Lord must be proud.

4 I told my coon
Jerusalem's
A land of milk and honey,
But I'd rather live
On Sour Cherry Ridge
And drink milk with my honey.

5 I asked my coon
What makes a boy
Go rarin' round the town,
And what makes a boy
Want to yell and scrap
And knock the other boys
down.

6 "Oh, coon," I said,
"I'm mighty glad
To have a coon like you,
For a coon won't tease
A boy like a girl,
Won't make a boy feel blue."

7 "Oh, coon," I said,
"If you marry me,
We'll raise the cutest chaps—
For it wouldn't s'prise me
If our kids were born
A-wearing coonskin caps!"

Gar went on:

> I told my coon
> The cherry tree
> With blossom now is bowed;
> If Heaven looks
> One half as fair,
> The good Lord must be proud.
>
> Coon, she says, a dillom-down,
> This coon named Barbary Allen.

Ma smiled to herself, for the song had taken a serious turn.

Gar sang on:

> I told my coon
> Jerusalem's
> A land of milk and honey,
> But I'd rather live
> On Sour Cherry Ridge
> And drink milk with my honey.
>
> Coon, she says, a dillom-down,
> This coon named Barbary Allen.

"It surely is a dancing song," Ash said, "with all those *dillom-downs.*"
Gar continued:

> I asked my coon
> What makes a boy
> Go rarin' round the town,
> And what makes a boy
> Want to yell and scrap
> And knock the other boys down.
>
> Coon, she says, a red-headed girl,
> A dillom-derry-down.

"Ah," Pa said.
Gar went right on:

> "Oh, coon," I said,
> "I'm mighty glad
> To have a coon like you,
> For a coon won't tease
> A boy like a girl,
> Won't make a boy feel blue."
>
> Coon, she says, a dillom-down,
> This coon named Barbary Allen.

By now everybody at the Song Swapping was joining in on the *dillom-downs*. And when that whole crowd sang, "This coon named Barbary Allen," Absalom could hear Barbary Allen making a loud chittering sound in his ear.

Looking straight at Absalom, Gar sang the last verse:

> "Oh, coon," I said,
> "If you marry me,
> We'll raise the cutest chaps—
> For it wouldn't s'prise me
> If our kids were born
> A-wearing coonskin caps!"
>
> Coon, she says, a dillom-down,
> This coon named Barbary Allen.

Then everybody at the Song Swapping bust out laughing. Crandall said he never heard anything so funny. Gavin said he never heard anything so fanciful. And Gar, when he'd finished, stole a look at Camden Pride, who was sitting next to Absalom. Camden Pride's cheeks were near the color of her red head, but you could tell the song was pleasing to her.

It was pleasing to other folks too. When Gar stepped down, everybody was nodding and clapping. For it was the kind of song to please man, woman, or child—those as favored love songs, and those as favored party songs or scrapping songs. It was the likeliest song Gar could have sung.

The Reverend Ben Jericho, who was judging, did not have to reckon long before he called out, "Mr. Gar Marvell—will he please to come forward and claim the hundred-dollar purse.

"This boy surely does have the sweet Marvell voice," Ben said as he handed Gar the purse. "But there never was a Marvell in this county that didn't sing like an angel."

"There's *one*," Gar said. And he reached down and lifted Absalom, coon and all, up onto the platform beside him.

"This boy has a voice rackety as a coon's," Gar said, grinning. "But it takes more than a sweet voice to make a good song. Don't I know it!"

And if Gar didn't lean over and kiss Barbary Allen, right in front of the whole Song Swapping! And the way people stomped then, you couldn't tell if it was for Gar or for Absalom's coon song.

Then Gar asked Absalom would Absalom hold the hundred-dollar purse while he stepped over to speak to Camden Pride.